Romeo's Guide to FREE London for Children

20 must-see sites and where kids can eat for FREE
Part 2

By Romeo Bremmer
Aged 11

**Romeo's Guide to
FREE London for Children**

20 must-see sites and where kids can eat for FREE
Part 2

First edition printed in 2019 in the United Kingdom
Copyright © 2019 Romeo Bremmer. All rights reserved.

Publishers: Bailey McKenzie & Juliet Coley
Text: Romeo Bremmer
Photographs: Yazmin McKenzie
Designer: Andy Pryor
Artworker: Becky Wybrow
Sub Editor: Jackie Raymond

A CIP catalogue record of this book is available from the British Library.
ISBN: (PBK) 978-1-9993274-7-7
All rights reserved

No part of this publication may be reproduced, stored in a retrieval system, or transmitted, in any form, or by any means, electrical, mechanical, photocopying, recording, or otherwise without the prior permission of the publication.

For orders or enquiries, contact:
BlackJac Media: 07429 481305
www.blackjacmedia.com
www.romeobremmer.com

This book is dedicated to all the staff and support staff at St Paul's with St Michael's Primary school, who made my school days simply the best! I'm going to miss you all. Thank you for all the AMAZING memories!

I also dedicate this book to all my friends who love to travel and enjoy themselves, especially
my Year 6 Classmates
Manhood Academy Crew
Haggerston
Football Team
& NTCOG Clapton Boys' Brigade Team

Love

Inside

5	**Dedication**
6	**Inside**
8	**Introduction**
9	*Parks, Playgrounds & Farms*
10	Golders Hill Park Zoo
12	St James's Park
14	The Regent's Park
16	Coram Fields & Queen Elizabeth Olympic Park
17	*Museums & Galleries*
18	Science Museum
20	The Saatchi Gallery
22	National History Museum
24	**Tube Map and Key**
26	Serpentine Gallery & National Portrait Gallery

Inside

27	*Attractions*
28	The Scoop
30	The Houses of Parliament
32	Trafalgar Square
34	Cass Art Saturday Workshops & DLR Driverless Trains
35	*My Favourites*
36	Leicester Square
38	British Library
40	Westfields London
42	Evergreen Playground & The Lego Store
43	Kids Eat Free
45	Thanks

Introduction

This is my fifth book and Part 2 of my *Guide to Free London for Children*. It builds on the idea of my second book: *'Romeo's Guide to London Architecture'*, but focuses on families and places kids can go to in London for FREE.

I had a fantastic time visiting all these places. London is a great place to live and visit, and has been named by the 2019 TripAdvisor Travellers' Choice awards as the best-rated destination in the world.

There is so much to see and do in London, and I focused on parks, playgrounds, farms, zoos, museums, galleries, popular London attractions and places that are my personal favourites. My favourites may not be obvious sightseeing locations, but places I love to go for free, like Westfields with my Mum; exploring the fun and exciting stores, or going with my sister on the Docklands Light Railway that does not have a driver!

I have also included places where kids can eat in London for free, however, with most offers an adult will have to buy a full price main course.

I hope you have as much fun as I did, planning and visiting the exciting places in my book.

Love

Romeo x

Parks, Playgrounds & Farms

Place:	Golders Hill Park Zoo
Type of Activity:	Zoo
Address:	West Heath Avenue, Golders Green, London NW11 7QP
Opening Times:	7.30am to dusk
Nearest Station:	Golders Green (2 minutes)
Telephone Number:	020 7332 3511
Website:	www.biaza.org.uk/members/detail/golders-hill-park-zoo

1

Golders Hill Park

Golders Hill Park Zoo is one of the only two free zoos in London. The zoo has a growing collection of rare and exotic birds and mammals, such as laughing kookaburras, ring-tailed lemurs and ring-tailed coatis. There is also a Butterfly House that is open from late March to October from 1pm to 3pm every day.

11

St James's Park

Place:	St James's Park
Type of Activity:	Park
Address:	London SW1A 2BJ
Opening Times:	5am to 12am midnight
Nearest Station:	Underground: Westminster (5 mins)
Telephone Number:	0300 061 2350
Website:	www.royalparks.org.uk/parks/st-jamess-park

2

12

St James's Park is one of London's eight Royal Parks and covers an area of nearly 57 acres. It includes The Mall and Horse Guards Parade, and is surrounded by landmarks, such as Buckingham Palace, Clarence House and Whitehall.

Visitors can see lovely views of the lake and fountain, or watch the resident pelicans at feeding time. Pelicans have lived in St James's Park for nearly 400 years. They were originally presented as a gift from the Russian Ambassador to King Charles II.

Regents Park

Place: The Regent's Park
Type of Activity: Park
Address: Chester Road, London NW1 4NR
Opening Times: 5am to 9.30pm
Nearest Station: Underground: Regent's Park (3 mins)
Telephone Number: 0300 061 2300
Website: www.royalparks.org.uk/parks/the-regents-park

The Regent's Park is one of London's eight Royal Parks and covers an area of 395 acres. It combines large open spaces, with four children's playgrounds. It is named after Prince Regent, sometimes known as the Playboy Prince, who later became King George IV (1762-1830).

You can walk through the flowerbeds in the Avenue Gardens and see more than 12,000 roses in Queen Mary's Gardens, or take a stroll up Primrose Hill for excellent views of the London skyline.

The park has a large wetland area, and is home to around 100 species of wild bird and a breeding population of hedgehogs.

Coram's Fields is a large urban open space, which occupies seven acres in Bloomsbury. It includes a children's playground, sand pits, a duck pond, a pets corner, café and nursery. Adults are only allowed to enter if they are accompanied by a child.

Queen Elizabeth Olympic Park is free to visit every day of the week. It's home to the London Stadium, the ArcelorMittal Orbit, the London Aquatics Centre, the Copper Box Arena, Lee Valley VeloPark and Lee Valley Hockey and Tennis Centre - as well as parklands, waterways, playgrounds and cafés. There is always something new to explore.

Coram's Fields & the Olympic Park 4 + 5

Place:	Coram's Fields
Type of Activity:	Playground
Address:	93 Guildford Street, London WC1N 1DN
Opening Times:	Open 363 days a year, closed Christmas and Boxing Day 9am to 5pm
Nearest Station:	Underground: Russell Square (5 mins)
Telephone Number:	020 7837 6138
Website:	www.coramsfields.org

Place:	Queen Elizabeth Olympic Park
Type of Activity:	Park
Address:	London E20 2ST
Opening Times:	24 hours a day, with limited lighting after dark
Nearest Station:	Underground: Stratford (18 mins)
:	Underground: Bow Road (19 mins)
Website:	https://www.queenelizabetholympicpark.co.uk

Museums & Galleries

Place:	Science Museum
Type of Activity:	Museum
Address:	Exhibition Road, Kensington, London SW7 2DD
Opening Times:	10am to 6pm. Closed 24th to 26th December
Nearest Station:	Underground: South Kensington (5 mins)
Telephone Number:	0333 241 4000
Website:	www.sciencemuseum.org.uk

6

The Science Museum

The Science Museum is an interactive science and technology museum. It is a great place to see, touch and experience science first hand.

There are over 15,000 objects on display, including world famous objects, such as the Apollo 10 Command Module and Stephenson's Rocket.

You can experience what it's like to fly with the Red Arrows, or blast off into space on an Apollo space mission, or watch a film on a screen taller than four double decker buses in the IMAX 3D Cinema.

Place:	Saatchi Gallery
Type of Activity:	Art Gallery
Address:	Cromwell Road, Kensington, London SW7 5BD
Opening Times:	10am to 5.50pm
Nearest Station:	Underground: South Kensington (4 mins)
Telephone Number:	020 7942 5511
Website:	www.saatchigallery.com

7

The Saatchi Gallery

The Saatchi Gallery is a gallery for contemporary art. It was opened by Charles Saatchi in 1985 so he could exhibit his art collection to the public.

The gallery has been an influence on art in Britain since its opening. It has provided a springboard to launch careers and many of the artists shown at the gallery are unknown to the general public and also to the commercial art world.

In 2010, it was announced that the gallery would be given to the British public, becoming the Museum of Contemporary Art for London.

The Natural History Museum

8

Place:	Natural History Museum
Type of Activity:	Museum
Address:	Cromwell Road, Kensington, London SW7 5BD
Opening Times:	10am to 5.50pm
Nearest Station:	Underground: South Kensington (4 mins)
Telephone Number:	020 7942 5511
Website:	www.nhm.ac.uk

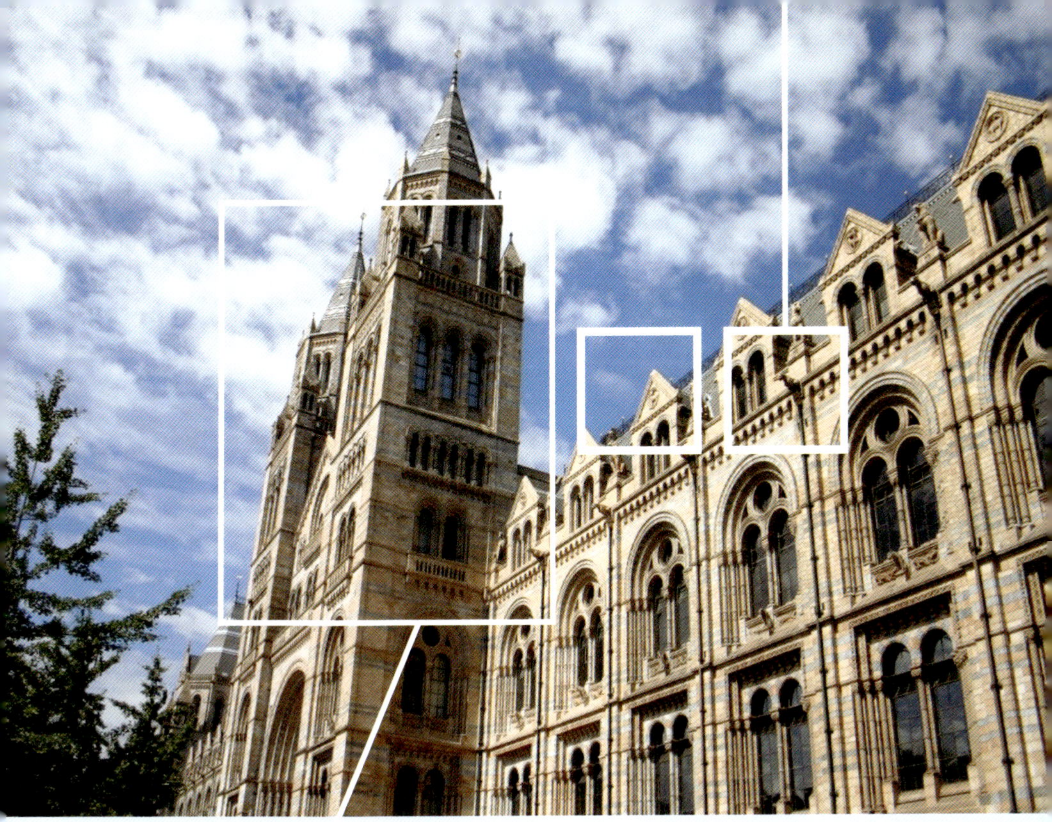

The Natural History Museum is a museum that exhibits a vast range of specimens from various segments of natural history.

The museum is home to life and earth science specimens, comprising of 80 million items within five main collections: botany, entomology, mineralogy, palaeontology and zoology.

Tube Map and Key

No.	Place	Tube Station
1	Golders Hill Park Zoo	Golders Green
2	St James's Park	St James Park
3	The Regent's Park	Regents Park
4	Coram Fields	Russell Square
5	Queen Elizabeth Olympic Park	Stratford
6	Science Museum	South Kensington
7	The Saatchi Gallery	Sloane Square
8	National History Museum	South Kensington
9	Serpentine Gallery	Lancaster Gate
10	National Portrait Gallery	Charing Cross
11	The Scoop	London Bridge
12	Houses of Parliament	Westminster
13	Forty Hall and Estate	Oakwood
14	Cass Art Saturday Workshops	Richmond
15	British Library	Euston
16	Leicester Square	Leicester Square
17	Trafalgar Square	Charing Cross
18	Westfields	Stratford/Shepherds Bush
19	DLR Driverless Trains	Bank
20	The Lego Store	Leicester Square
21	The Real Greek, Bankside	London Bridge
22	The Real Greek, Covent Garden	Covent Garden
23	The Real Greek, Muswell Hill	Highgate
24	The Real Greek, Dulwich	Brixton
25	The Real Greek, Marylebone	Baker Street
26	The Real Greek, Soho	Oxford Street
27	The Real Greek, Spitalfields	Liverpool Street
28	The Real Greek, St Martin's Lane	Leicester Square
29	The Real Greek, Westfield Stratford	Stratford
30	The Real Greek, Westfield London	Shepherds Bush
31	Bodean, Old Street	Old Street
32	Bodean, Balham	Balham
33	Bodean, Clapham	Clapham Common
34	Bodean, Tower Hill	Tower Hill
35	Morrisons In Store Café	Stratford
		Camden Town
		Acton
		Edgeware

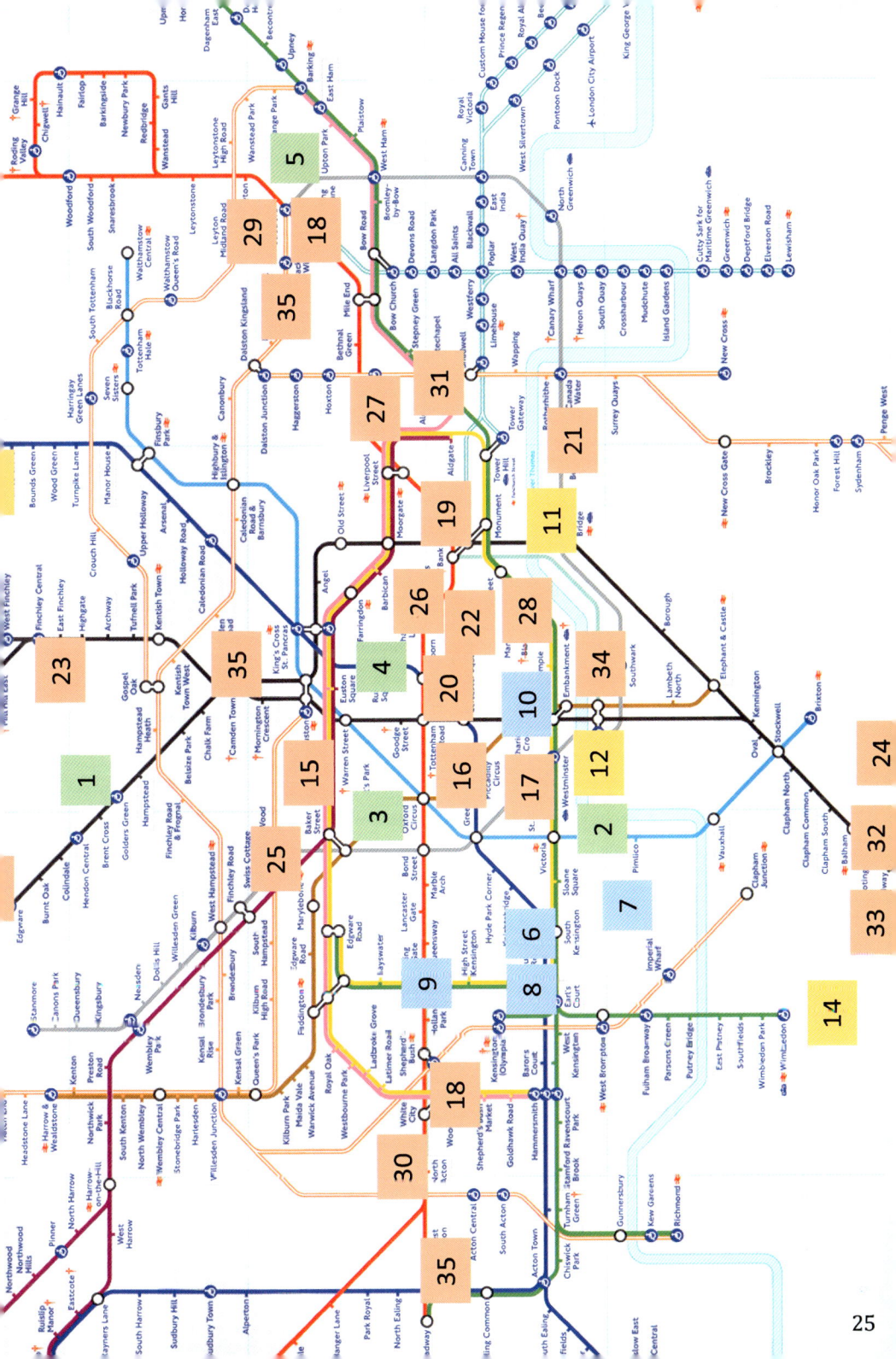

Place:	Serpentine Galleries
Type of Activity:	Art Gallery
Address:	Kensington Gardens, London W2 3XA
Opening Times:	Tuesday to Sunday, 10am to 6pm
Nearest Station:	Underground: Charing Cross (4 mins)
Telephone Number:	020 7402 6075
Website:	www.serpentinegalleries.org

Place:	National Portrait Gallery
Type of Activity:	Art Gallery
Address:	St Martin's Place, London WC2H 0HE
Opening Times:	10am to 6pm, Sunday to Thursday, 10am to 9pm, Friday
Nearest Station:	Underground: Charing Cross (4 mins), Leicester Square (6 mins)
Telephone Number:	020 7306 0055
Website:	www.npg.org.uk

The Serpentine & the National Portrait Gallery

The Serpentine Galleries are two contemporary art galleries in Kensington Gardens, Hyde Park. The galleries were established in 1970, and showcase emerging and established contemporary art and architecture. The Serpentine Gallery and the Serpentine Sackler Gallery are within five minutes' walk of each other, linked by the bridge over the Serpentine Lake.

The National Portrait Gallery is an art gallery in London that has a large collection of historical portraits and portraits of famous British people. It was the first portrait gallery in the world when it opened in 1856.

9 + 10

Attractions

Place:	The Scoop
Type of Activity:	Open-air venue space
Address:	London Bridge City, London SE1 2DB
Opening Times:	Varies, depending on individual events
Nearest Station:	Underground: London Bridge (5 mins)
Telephone Number:	020 7403 4866
Website:	www.london-se1.co.uk/places/scoop

11

The Scoop

thescoop
at More London

Catch free theatre, festivals, films and sports screening by the river at this spectacular outdoor amphitheatre.

It has 800 seats and is situated next to London's City Hall on the south bank of the Thames, close to Tower Bridge.

From June to August, you can enjoy a variety of free events, as part of the London Bridge City Summer Festival, including sports screenings, films, music and theatre, as well as riverside food and drink. Arrive early to secure your spot.

Place:	Houses of Parliament
Type of Activity:	Offices for British Members of Parliament
Address:	Westminster, London SW1A 0AA
Opening Times:	Monday to Friday, 9am to 5pm
Nearest Station:	Underground: Westminster (1 min)
Telephone Number:	020 7219 3000
Website:	www.parliament.uk

12

The Houses of Parliament

The business of Parliament takes place in two Houses: the House of Commons and the House of Lords. This is where they make laws, check the work of the government and debate current issues.

The UK Parliament is open to visitors all year round, Monday to Saturday, to attend debates and committee hearings, or to take a tour of one of the world's most iconic buildings.

Trafalgar Square

13

Place:	Trafalgar Square
Type of Activity:	Tourist Monument
Address:	London WC2N 5DN
Opening Times:	24 hours a day
Nearest Station:	Charing Cross (1 min)
Telephone Number:	020 7983 4750
Website:	www.london.gov.uk

This Square is like a large and lively playground. It is surrounded by pigeons and, even though you are not allowed to feed them, you can climb on the huge bronze lions (if you are not scared of heights!), or splash about in the fountains on a hot summer day.

You can also see a replica of Lamassu (a winged bull with human head) on the Fourth Plinth. The work will stay on display until 2020.

33

Place:	Cass Art Saturday Workshops
Type of Activity:	Art Workshops
Address:	103 Clarence Street, Kingston, London KT1 1QY
Opening Times:	10am to 12pm
Nearest Station:	Overground: Kingston (3 mins)
Telephone Number:	020 7619 2601
Website:	www.cassart.co.uk

Place:	DLR Driverless Trains
Type of Activity:	Transport Ride
Address:	The DLR runs through London from Stratford to Woolwich Arsenal
Opening Times:	5.30am to 12.30am
Nearest Station:	Any station on the DLR route
Telephone Number:	0343 222 1234
Website:	www.dlrlondon.co.uk

The Docklands Light Railway & Cass Art Workshop

14 + 15

The Docklands Light Railway (DLR) is an automated light metro system that opened in 1987 to serve the redeveloped Docklands area of East London. The system uses minimal staffing on trains and at major interchange stations. The four below-ground stations are staffed to comply with underground station fire and safety requirements. I pretend to be a train driver by sitting in the front carriage of the 'driverless' train.

Cass Art Workshop's creative drop-in inspires and triggers children's imaginations. The minimum age is four years old, children must be accompanied by an adult, and all materials are provided. Places are on a first come, first served basis.

My Favourites

Place:	Leicester Square
Type of Activity:	Tourist Area
Address:	Leicester Square, London WC2H 0AP
Opening Times:	24 hours a day
Nearest Station:	Underground: Leicester Square (0 min walk)
Telephone Number:	020 7420 5856
Website:	www.leicestersquarelondon

16

Leicester Square

The buzz of London can be found in and around this Square. If you're lucky, you can meet international celebrities at a red carpet premiere, and enjoy a lovely meal in nearby restaurants. Any child can eat for free at Angus Steakhouse between 12pm and 5pm, with a full paying adult. What I enjoy most about Leicester Square are the shops. I have spent hours having fun in M&M's World and the Lego Store, which are massive, and I have not spent a penny.

37

17
The British Library

Place:	The British Library
Type of Activity:	Library
Address:	96 Euston Road, London NW1 2DB
Opening Times:	Monday to Thursday, 9.30am to 8pm
	Friday, 9.30am to 8pm Saturday, 9.30am to 8pm
	Sunday, 11.30am to 5pm
Nearest Station:	Underground: Kings Cross (6 mins)
Telephone Number:	0330 333 1144
Website:	www.bl.uk

The British Library is the national library of the United Kingdom, and the largest national library in the world by the number of items catalogued. It is estimated to contain 150-200 million items from many countries. As a legal deposit library, the British Library receives copies of all books produced in the United Kingdom and Ireland, including my four books: *'Life Without My Mummy?'*, *'Romeo's guide to London Architecture'*, *'Romeo's Guide to Free London for Children'* and *'Hey, Black Boy!'*.

Westfield Shopping Centre

18

Place:	Westfield London
Type of Activity:	Shopping Centre
Address:	Stratford City, Montfichet Road, Olympic Park, E20 1EJ
	Shepherd's Bush, Ariel Way, White City, W12 7GF
Opening Times:	10am to 10pm
Nearest Station:	WSC: Underground: Stratford (4 mins)
	WSB: Underground: Shepherd's Bush (3 mins)
Telephone Number:	020 8371 2300
Website:	https://uk.westfield.com/london

Westfield London is fashion, food, leisure and entertainment for all the family under one roof.

It has a calendar of free arts and educational events, and I love spending time in my favourite shops looking at my favourite items of clothing and trainers, and playing with the exciting toys and new products.

Every Saturday, from 10am 11am, there is a Quiet Hour, as Westfield has joined the global #LightItUpBlue campaign in support of #WorldAutismAwarenessDay

Place:	Holly Street Adventure Playground
Type of Activity:	Adventure Playground
Address:	Beehive Close, Dalston, London E8 3JT
Opening Times:	Term Time: Tues to Fri: 4pm to 7pm
	Saturday: 12pm to 5pm
	School Holidays: Mon to Fri: 10am to 5pm
Nearest Station:	Overground: Haggerston Station (10 mins)
Telephone Number:	0207 275 9004

Place:	The Lego Store
Type of Activity:	Toy Shop and Activity Centre
Address:	3 Swiss Court, London W1D 6AP
Opening Times:	Mon to Sat 10am to 10pm, Sunday 12pm to 6pm
Nearest Station:	Underground: Leicester Square (4 mins)
Telephone Number:	020 7839 3480
Website:	www.lego.com/en-gb

Evergreen Adventure Playground & the Lego Store

Evergreen, known locally as Holly Street Adventure offer free, fun, supervised adventure play for all children aged 5 to15 years. You pay a £1 registration fee but after that, after school and school holidays play is free.

The Lego Store in Leicester Square is the biggest store anywhere in the world! It is on two floors, and has 914 square metres of Lego. One feature is a huge 6.53 metre working Lego model of London's famous Big Ben that lights up at night.

19 + 20

The Real Greek
Food Type:
Address: Bankside: 2a Southwark Bridge Road, SE1 9HA
Covent Garden: 60-62 Long Acre, WC2E 9JE
Muswell Hill: 224 Muswell Hill Broadway, N10 3SH
Dulwich: 96-98 Dulwich Village, SE21 7AQ
Marylebone: 56 Paddington Street, W1U 4HY
Soho: 50 Berwick Street, W1F 8SJ
Spitalfields: 6 Horner Square, E1 6EW
St Martin's Lane: 54 St Martin's Lane, WC2N 4EA
Westfield Stratford: 2 Chestnut Plaza, Montfichet Road, E20 1GL
Westfield London: Southern Terrace, Ariel Way, W12 7GB
Telephone No: Bread Street: 020 3030 4050, Heddon Street: 020 7592 1212
Website: www.therealgreek.com
Days: Sundays
Times: All day
Any Conditions: Free kids meal with every £10 spent on a adult meal on Sundays. Dine-in only. Not valid with any other offer or promotion.

Bodean's BBQ
Food Type: American BBQ
Address: Old Street: 201 City Road, London EC1V 1JN
Balham: 225 Balham High Road, London SW17 7BQ
Clapham: 169 Clapham High Street, London SW4 7SS
Tower Hill: 16 Byward Street, London EC3R 5BA
Telephone No: Old Street: 020 7608 7230, Balham: 020 8682 4650
Clapham: 020 7622 4248, Tower Hill: 020 7488 3883
Website: www.bodeansbbq.com
Days: Monday to Sunday
Times: Up to 3pm on weekdays and 5pm on weekends
Any Conditions: Under 16s eat free with a full-paying adult

Morrison's In Store Café
Food Type: British and modern European
Address: Morrison stores with cafés
Telephone No: 0345 611 6111
Website: www.mymorrisons.com
Days: Every day, all day
Times: All day when café is open
Any Conditions: One free children's meal when you buy an adult meal over £4.50 or a breakfast meal over £3.50

Kids Eat Free at Morrisons & The Real Greek

Thanks

My first Thank You goes to the Lord God Almighty.

Also massive thanks go to: Bailey McKenzie, Juliet Coley, Yazmin McKenzie, Lilieth Coley-Wright, Kenneth Bremmer, Lyz Bailey, Mark Bailey, Julia Bailey, Marcia Dixon, Andy Pryor and Jackie Raymond.

Not forgetting: Grandma Dell, Tarnnia, Mama Gem, Carmen, Josh, Royston (RIP), Benson, Aunty Joan, Aunty Antoinette, Uncle Tony, Reana, Jordan, Lanette, Aunty Liz, Uncle Wayne, Uncle Kevin, Uncle Roland, Uncle Nicky, Kieron, Adisa, Aunty Dorothy, Aunty Ade, Aunty Odette, Aunty Jenny, Aunty Denice and Aunty Paulette.

And all the children in my family who will benefit from visiting these great places in my book: Camal, Liana, Ziah, Iyana, Imaya, Akaii, Kairo, Nia, Tiarn, King, LeShawn, Hakiem, Karis, Kalil, Keon, Mollie and Jamari.

Plus my New Testament Assembly church family, my NTCOG Boys Brigade Leaders O'Neil and Lionel, all the role models at Manhood Academy, the wonderful staff at St Paul's with St Michael's: Ms Lot, Miss Markland, Mr Ryan, Ms Komer, Ms Haq, Ms Foster, Ms Spencer, Ms Longva, Ms Hoy, Ms Porteous, Mr Gonzalez, Ms Moroney, Ms Lekka, Janet, Chris, Pam, Christine, Brian, Alex, Ria, Paul, Tyla, Coleen, Sheldon, Rahana, Rana and Ms Murray.

Not forgetting my fantastic Year 6 classmates who, after seven years are moving on to the next step of our exciting school journey:

Casey, Riley R, Ella-Jae, Cece, Aliyah B, Emmanuel, Aaliyah R, Ryan, Sophia G, Nathan, Marie, Riley D, Destiny, Samuel, Aydin, Jesse, Tyler, Pinar, Vinee, Keziah, Sophia MS, Ella T, Regina, Setyra, Erin, Hailey, Ednessa and Felicity.

And those who left SPSM but had a great influence on me: Ms Olufiade, Mr Bergin, Ms Rose, Ms Jessop, Ms Bunbury, Trevor, Kim, Alison, Gabriel, Laura and Mr Tom Panagiotopoulos - you are still a SPSM. ☺

Books by Romeo Bremmer

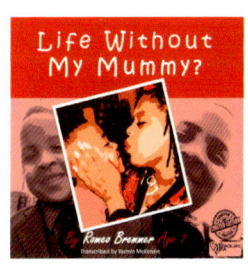 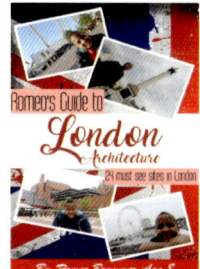  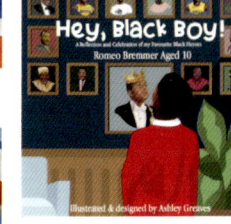

Life Without My Mummy? by Romeo Bremmer, aged 7
ISBN: 978-0-9933168-0-7

"Romeo captured my heart with this moving account in
'Life Without My Mummy? Mummy?' which tells of when
he nearly lost his mum, Juliet."
Marcia Dixon, *The Voice* newspaper

Winner of TruLittle Hero Scribe of the Year 2016

Romeo's Guide to London Architecture by Romeo Bremmer, aged 8
ISBN: 978-0-9933168-5-2

Romeo's Guide to Free London for Children by Romeo Bremmer, aged 9
ISBN: 978-1-9993274-5-3

Hey, Black Boy! by Romeo Bremmer, aged 10
ISBN: 978-0-9933168-8-3

"The inspiration behind *'Hey, Black Boy!'* is remarkable! It will inspire
many young people on the importance of identity, and Romeo's age
suggests we will be seeing much more of his brilliance."
Paul McKenzie, Director of Soapbox, Real Talking Inspiration

Winner of TruLittle Hero Scribe of the Year 2018
For more information and to order, visit:
www.blackjacmedia.com
www.romeobremmer.com

**WINNER
2016**

**WINNER
2018**